Just Plain Bob

Cyndi
Intense Erotica

WARNING

This book contains sexually explicit scenes and adult language. It may be considered offensive to some readers. This book is for sale to adults ONLY.

Please store your files wisely where they cannot be accessed by underage readers.

* * * * * * * * * * * * * * * * * * * *

WANT FREE COPIES OF MY BOOKS?

Just visit my blog and download free copies of my books:

awesomeauthors.org/justplainbob

About the Publisher

4Fun Publishing, a member of **BLVNP Incorporated**, 340 S. Lemon #6200, Walnut CA 91789, info@blvnp.com / legal@blvnp.com
NOTE: Due to the highly emotional reaction of some people to works of erotic fiction, any email sent to the above address that contains foul language or religious references is automatically deleted by our anti-spam software and will not be seen. All other communications are welcome.

DISCLAIMER

Please don't be stupid and kill yourself. This book is a work of FICTION. Do not try any new sexual practice that you find in this book. It is fiction and not to be confused with reality. Neither the author nor the publisher or its associates assume any responsibility for any loss, injury, death or legal consequences resulting from acting on the contents in this book. Every character in this book is over 18 years of age. The author's opinions are not to be construed as the opinions of the publisher. The material in this book is for entertainment purposes ONLY. Enjoy.

Cyndi

Intense Erotica

By: Just Plain Bob

ISBN: 978-1-68030-450-3

CHAPTER 1

My sister was getting married and I had to fly back to Michigan for the wedding. I was running a little late for the flight and I didn't have time to stop and browse the magazine rack for something to read on the flight. Once we were airborne, I checked the seat pockets on my row and I found a well-thumbed copy of Gallery magazine. I ended up reading it from cover to cover, but what grabbed me was the section called Feedback. It had half a dozen letters from guys who got turned on from watching their wives get it on with other men. One in particular really got to me, it was from a guy who set up gangbangs for his wife and then ate her out after all the guys were done with her. The eating her out part didn't appeal to me, but I started having thoughts about what my sexy wife would look like in the throes of passion being serviced by other guys. The idea turned me on so much that my dick stayed hard the entire flight to Detroit.

Luckily, Cyndi had flown back a couple of days ahead of me and was going to be meeting my flight; and considering how hard my dick was, I was seriously considering that we might just have to get it on in the car in the parking lot. Any thoughts of having Cyndi take care of my problem died as I came down the ramp and saw her waiting for me with my mother and sister. We did get it on later that night, but with nowhere near the intensity that would have been there just after the flight.

***

As charged up as I was after reading that copy of Gallery, it all faded during the hectic week that followed and it wasn't until the flight home that the charge built up again. This time I was early for the flight and as I checked out the magazine racks at the terminal I spotted the latest issue of Gallery and I bought it. I also noticed a magazine that had "Hot Wives" on the cover and I bought it too. It turned out to be Penthouse Letters and it was even hotter than the first Gallery that I had read. My wife, who was traveling with me this time, had occasion to reach across me for something and her wrist hit my erection. She stopped and cupped my hard cock with her hand and smiled:

"Is that for me?"

"As soon as we get home my sweet, just as soon as we get home."

She gave me a squeeze and asked me what caused it and I showed her the cover of the magazine I was reading.

"I want to read it when you get done. If it does this," and she gave me another squeeze, "for you, I wonder what it will do for me."

I know what I'm hoping it will do, I thought. I passed her the Penthouse when I was done and I picked up the Gallery, and as I read it, I kept glancing at Cyndi out of the corner of my eye to see how she was reacting. All I saw was concentration and she never once betrayed what she might be thinking.

On the ride home from the airport, Cyndi was not her usual talkative self and I commented on it. She gave me a look that I couldn't decipher and said:

"I'm sitting here wondering if I should be worrying about you, or maybe more to the point, worrying about us."

"In what way?" I asked.

"Well, you got a hard-on from reading that magazine, but when I read it all, I found there were sections on anal sex, domination, homosexuality, swinging and swapping and one on watching your wife have sex with other men. The section on anal sex shouldn't have much of an effect on you because we have practiced anal sex since we started dating. That leaves the other four and if one of those excites you then we have a problem because all of them leave me cold."

Discretion being the better part of valor, I lied.

"Actually it was the picture of the big-titted blonde with the black cock in her hand that got to me."

Cyndi burst out laughing, "You never could lie worth a shit. I know you are not gay, and I'm betting that domination would turn you off so that leaves swapping or watching. Which is it?"

I was quiet for a bit before saying, "Watching."

She looked at me in surprise and then said, "No way Jose, not this lady! No way I'm going to take on another guy so you can hide in the closet and watch."

"Actually" I said, "I was thinking more along the lines of a group of guys, maybe five or six."

She just shook her head and said, "I don't believe this, but it doesn't matter because it ain't never going to happen!"

***

That was two years ago and since that time I've read every issue of Penthouse Letters that has come out and the letters keep the fantasy alive in my mind. Every letter I read has Cyndi in the starring role and the image of her being fucked by other men has never failed to give me a raging hard-on. Between masturbating to those images and chasing Cyndi all over the house for a week after every new issue comes out, my dick hovers on the borderline between sore and just plain tired. But the bottom line has always been that it was never going to happen.

***

Then, on one momentous day, the stars in the heavens fell into perfect alignment and caused several things to fall into place at the same time. All that was needed to make things happen was for me to be an asshole. Normally, or at least I liked to think it, I would not have done what I did, but it just happened to be the day after I'd received and read from cover to cover the latest issue of Penthouse Letters. The images of Cyndi being the one fucked in all those letters was still dancing in my mind when the circumstances all fell into place and I went for it.

We were throwing a promotion party for one of my co-workers and everyone was having a great time. Cyndi looked great as usual, and as always, she got a great deal of attention, especially from the single guys. Cyndi was also totally bombed, which was rare since she hardly ever drank. When she did, she became a silly drunk and a drunk who got giggly and who thought everything was funny. For about an hour, I'd noticed Cyndi dancing with a small group of guys and once or twice I'd seen a few cop a feel or two. One of the guys who had the busiest hands was Jerry, a guy I knew pretty well and liked. I took a stiff drink to fortify myself, knowing that what I was going to do could backfire on me, and then I went over to talk to Jerry.

"You know what I like about you, Jerry?" I asked, "You are almost as big an asshole as me."

He laughed and said, "When you're right, you're right!" and we clicked glasses.

"In fact" I went on, "You are the kind of asshole who would take my drunken wife up to the master bedroom and fuck her if you got the chance. And all it would probably take would be for me to disappear for a bit."

Jerry gave me a strange look and then you could almost see the light bulb go off above his head. He smiled and said:

"When you're right, you're right!" and we clinked glasses again.

Then I said, "I think we are almost out of beer and I'm going to have to make a beer run" and I walked off and left him. I circulated among the guests and let them know I was going to make a beer run and then I went out and moved my car down the street and then went back to the house.

My house was built in the 'thirties' when things were done differently than they are now. I have two staircases to the upstairs, one in the foyer, and the one to the kitchen that the servants used to use to take breakfast upstairs to the family in residence. I came in the back door and went up to the bedroom and got into (where else?) the closet. I arranged things so I could watch comfortably and then I waited.

It wasn't long before the bedroom door opened and a giggling Cyndi came in followed by Jerry. Cyndi turned to face him and said:

"Okay, here we are. What did you want to show me?"

Jerry didn't say a word, he just opened his fly and took out his hard cock. Cyndi giggled and said:

"You can't do that. You are not my husband so you can't do that. Only he can do that."

Jerry walked toward her, dick jutting out in front of him and Cyndi took a step backward, stumbled and ended up sitting on the edge of the bed which put her head on the same level as Jerry's cock. He kept walking toward her and she, still giggling drunkenly, put her hands up to ward him off.

"Jerry, stop this silliness now. Rob wouldn't like this at all. Now just put that thing away and go back do..." and her words were cut off by Jerry's cock going into her mouth.

Cyndi's little fists started beating on Jerry's legs and she was trying to push her away, but he had his hands on the back of her head and he started to fuck her mouth. She just sat there as Jerry face-fucked her and then slowly her hands came up and gripped his ass. Jerry dropped his hands and stopped face-fucking Cyndi, but Cyndi didn't stop sucking on him.

After a couple of minutes, Jerry pulled his cock out of her mouth and in one quick motion, he bent down, grabbed her legs, flipped her back on the bed and before she knew it, he had her skirt up to her waist, her panties off and he had moved on top of her into a position to do a sixty-nine. She started to protest, but when she opened her mouth, Jerry's cock slipped into the open hole.

"No, no, you can't. You mustn't. Please stop; please don't do this to me."

But Jerry didn't listen; he just kept eating her pussy. After a couple of minutes, Cyndi went strangely silent and then she opened her legs as far as she could, planted her feet and pushed her pussy up at Jerry's mouth. The sobbing had been replaced by a long low moan followed by a series of little cries, Cyndi's signal that she was having an orgasm. And then, wonder of wonders, she turned her head and took Jerry's dick back into her mouth. Her full red lips clamped around Jerry's cock was the most erotic thing I had ever seen. Jerry pumped her mouth a couple of times and then he swung around and moved between Cyndi's legs. When his cock was pulled out of her mouth, her head followed it up and she tried to capture it again, a dazed expression on her face.

As Jerry drove his cock into her, she exhaled in a loud grunt as if Jerry's cock had pushed all the air out of her lungs, her eyes got big and the look on her face fairly screamed out:

"What's happening to me?"

Jerry was fucking her in earnest now, long hard strokes that were touching something inside Cyndi because she was arching her back and pushing her pussy up at him. He fucked her for a good five minutes and Cyndi had two more orgasms before Jerry finally said:

"Are you safe? You on the pill or have your diaphragm in?"

Cyndi hissed out a yes and Jerry let go his load. Cyndi cried out, "Not yet, oh please god not yet, finish me, I'm almost there, finish me."

But Jerry was limp. I saw him glance quickly at the closet (I wondered if he would figure that out) and then he got up and left the room. I watched as Cyndi tried to get herself off using her fingers, but she hadn't managed by the time Jerry got back - and he wasn't alone! He had George with him, another guy I work with.

Cyndi was so busy trying to get herself off that she hadn't noticed the two men come into the room. The first she was aware of it was when George pushed her hand out of the way and pushed his cock in her. Her initial reaction was, "Oh god yes, fuck me, please fuck me," and then her eyes popped open and she saw it wasn't Jerry and she began to frantically search the room until her eyes landed on Jerry and then she seemed to calm down.

By then George was pounding away and soon the low moans and the little cries began again and Cyndi was thrashing around on the bed, her hips pushing up at George. Jerry had his cock back out and it was hard again and as soon as George finished, Jerry took his place for a second go round. The sight was unbelievably erotic and I had already cum twice and I was still whipping a hard cock. I was more turned on by what I was seeing than I would have believed possible. I was so busy watching Jerry fuck my wife and beating my meat that I didn't see George leave, but I noticed when he came back because he had two more guys with him. They stood and watched as Jerry pounded away and then George said:

"Who wants to be next?"

Both men dropped their trousers and were stepping out of them when Jerry finished and his dick wasn't completely out of Cyndi before Dave was shoving him out of the way and then shoving his cock in Cyndi. I don't think Cyndi even noticed the change. Dave was followed by Tom, who was followed by George, who was followed by Dave again, and then the bedroom door opened and Ray, my boss, came in and closed the door behind him. Jerry said:

"Christ, Ray, your wife is downstairs." And Ray laughed and said, "Who do you think it was who told me what was going on up here? She told me if I wanted some, I should hurry up and that she would watch for Rob and holler when she saw him coming."

He was buried to the hilt in Cyndi before Dave was all the way out of the way. There it was! What I had always pictured in my mind: Cyndi with a group of guys fucking her, and I was loving it. And more to the point, she was too, if her begging to be fucked was any indication. Jerry did her one more time and then Ray took seconds and still Cyndi lay there moaning:

"Fuck me, please fuck me."

Jerry left the room and came back a few minutes later with a digital camera and began taking pictures of the guys fucking Cyndi. George asked him what he was doing and Jerry said:

"I don't want to wait for the next time she gets drunk and Rob isn't around. I'll give her call in a couple of days or so, show her the pictures and tell her we want to get together again. If she balks, I'll threaten to show Rob the pictures."

Cheers from everyone greeted this and then Ray said he wanted a set, "I've got a few ideas for Cyndi too."

Strangely, none of this upsets me. It meant that I would get to see Cyndi get group-fucked again. After Jerry was done taking pictures, George said:

"We need to get her cleaned up before Rob gets back."

The rest of the group got dressed while Jerry and George helped Cyndi into the bathroom. The rest of the guys left and I waited a minute or two and then I peeked out to see if the coast was clear. Jerry and George were still in the bathroom with Cyndi and everyone else was gone so I hurried out of the room and beat it down the back stairs and got out of the house without being seen.

Five minutes later, I was walking in the front door as Ray, his wife; Jerry and George were getting ready to leave. I gave them a bullshit story about having a flat tire and finding that the spare was flat also and having to wait for AAA. Jerry told me that Cyndi was a little under the weather and so they took her up and put her to bed. Ray's wife said:

"The poor dear had a very hard night," and I knew the bitch was just being catty by the way she emphasized the word 'hard'.

I had planned on being the last one to fuck Cyndi that night, but when I got to the bedroom, she was sound asleep and snoring. Oh well, I thought, there's always tomorrow.

***

I was the first one up the next morning and to set the stage, or prime the pump so to speak, I was sitting at the table sipping coffee and reading the latest issue of Penthouse Letters when Cyndi came down. She poured herself a cup of coffee and I waited for her to tell me about her night of lust. Instead, she looked at the magazine and said:

"Why are you still reading that stuff? You don't still think of me doing stuff like that, do you?"

The look on my face told her that I did and she said, "Sorry. It just isn't going to happen. I'm strictly a one-man woman, baby, learn to live with it."

I sat there in total surprise. It had never occurred to me that she wouldn't tell me about her night. I had expected her to say something like:

"Guess what? Your fantasy came true last night, but you weren't here to see it."

But to hide it from me? I just looked at her and thought to myself, "Okay, if that's the way you want to play it, I'll just have to try something else."

And I did, but that's another story.

CHAPTER 2

The first person I saw when I got to work on Monday was Jerry. He came into my office and said:

"I came to see if you were pissed off at me."

"For what?" I asked.

"For getting your wife done by all those other guys"

"Well," I said, "It was more than I expected, but no harm done. After her initial reluctance, she seemed to be having a good time, but it didn't turn out the way I thought it would."

Jerry sat down in the chair across from me and asked, "What do you mean, just what did you expect?"

I told him about my fantasies and how I thought if I got her fucked by another man and she enjoyed it, she would indulge me.

"What happen?" he asked.

"She never said a word about what happened and, in fact, when she saw me reading PHL the next morning, she told me to get used to the fact that she would never consider doing something like that."

"Oh well," he said as he got up to leave, "At least you got to see it once."

He turned to leave and then stopped and turned back toward me; taking an envelope from his pocket he said:

"Here," and handed it to me. "It's the disc from the digital camera. I don't know why, but when we were all fucking Cyndi, the idea came to me that you might like some pictures."

The light bulb went off above my head and I handed him back the envelope, "You keep it," I said.

He gave me a look that asked "Why?"

I smiled, "I seem to remember you telling the guys you were going to use the pictures to blackmail Cyndi into getting together with all of you again. I think that's a good idea. And when it happens, I'll be there to watch. One thing though; no one but you and me are ever to know I'm there."

***

Cyndi worked as a consultant and the majority of the time she worked out of our house. She would usually visit her clients in the morning and then come home around noon and work on the computer the rest of the day. Tuesday, Jerry and I put my scheme into motion. I came home around eleven and waited until Cyndi came home before getting into the closet. I called Jerry on my cellphone and told him she was home and five minutes, he rang the doorbell. Cyndi opened the door, but did not ask him in:

"What do you want?" she asked.

"Well, we had so much fun the other night that I wanted to do it again."

"In your dreams, asshole," Cyndi said, "You took advantage of me that night and got away with it, but it isn't ever going to happen again."

Jerry smiled at her and took the pictures out of his pocket and handed her one, "I'm going to take advantage of you again, and again, and again. That is, unless you don't care if Rob sees these pictures. He will just come to work one day and find them sitting on his desk."

Cyndi was silent for several moments and then she stepped back and let Jerry in. Five minutes later, Cyndi was lying naked on the bed with her legs spread wide and saying to Jerry, "Okay, asshole, let's get it over with," and five minutes later she was begging him to fuck her harder.

I watched her fuck him, suck him hard again, and then fuck him some more. Each time he got up to leave, she pulled him back down, got him hard and fucked him again. It was four thirty in the afternoon before Cyndi said:

"You have to go. I need to clean up and put clean sheets on the bed before Rob gets home."

As Jerry was leaving he said, "I'll call you."

"What for?"

"Because you and I are going to be doing this again - lots."

"You bastard!" Cyndi said as she slammed the door behind him.

While Cyndi was showing Jerry out, I hurried down the back stairs and out of the house. I was waiting for Jerry at the Landing Strip, a local bar about six blocks from the house.

"You got some woman there, Rob. If you had been out of town, I don't know that she would have let me leave."

"Maybe some other time I'll do that for you, but for now, we need to set up the next time. It's got to be somewhere where I can watch and I want you to have all the guys who did her the other night there, too.

***

Thursday at two, I was already in the closet at Jerry's when the rest of the guys began arriving. The doorbell rang at two fifteen and Jerry had all the guys move into the bedroom before he answered the door. Cyndi thought she was just coming to see Jerry and the others were going to be a surprise. I could hear the conversation as Cyndi came in:

"How long do you plan on doing this?" she asked.

"Until I get tired of you," Jerry said, "And that could be a long, long time."

"You really are a low life. Okay, let's get it over with."

I could hear them walking toward the bedroom where the guys were naked and waiting. The surprise, followed by the resignation on Cyndi's face, almost caused me to come out of the closet and put a stop to things. For about a tenth of a second. Then I considered that she wouldn't be here at all if she wasn't hiding things from me. She stood in the doorway and surveyed the room and then with a blank expression on her face, she walked over to the bed and took off her clothes. Once naked, she laid down on the bed and in a voice absolutely devoid of emotion said:

"Don't just fucking stand there. I haven't got all day. Who's first?"

The guys looked at each other and I could almost read their minds, "This isn't the laughing, giggly woman from the other night. This probably isn't even going to be fun. She'll probably just lay there like a blow up doll."

Jerry stepped forward and Cyndi spread her legs wide, but Jerry didn't do what she expected him to do. He went to his knees and started to eat her pussy. I could see in her face that she was determined not to show any emotion, that she was going to rob these guys of a willing sexual partner. She was just going to lay there passive and unresponding until they were done. Her resolved slowly faded as Jerry worked on her love button with his tongue and pumped her pussy with his fingers. Jerry had Cyndi moaning in about two minutes and in another minute or so, Cyndi was begging for someone to please fuck her.

The next three hours passed way too quickly for me as the guys fucked Cyndi one after another and as she begged and pleaded for more cock. She was never without a cock in her mouth or cunt for more than a minute during the entire time. Every guy there fucked Cyndi twice and Jerry and George fucked her three times. At five thirty, Jerry told everyone that it was time to go:

"We have to see that the little lady gets home in time to fix her hubby his dinner. We don't want to ruin a good thing, right?"

Cyndi was lying on the bed breathing hard when Jerry came back into the bedroom. He walked over to her and pushed his limp cock against Cyndi's mouth and it opened and took him in. In minutes, Cyndi had him hard again and he climbed on the bed and started to roll her over on her stomach.

"What are you doing?" she asked.

Jerry laughed and said "There's one hole that hasn't been used yet and I want to try it."

Cyndi pulled away from him and said, "No! I've got to keep something that's just Rob's. No one goes there except Rob!"

I do have to admit that I was touched by that little display of indignation. Jerry said:

"Honey. You don't get a choice. Remember the pictures?"

Cyndi was hot now, "Fuck you and those fucking pictures. If you are willing to throw away what you already have over something that you are not ever going to get, you are too stupid to be seen with!" and she jumped out of bed and gathered up her clothes.

The importance of what she had just said hit Jerry and me at the same time. She had just agreed to let herself be fucked whenever Jerry wanted, but only as long as her asshole was off limits. After she was gone, Jerry and I sat down and decided when we were going to do it next. We decided that once a week would be enough (except for Jerry - he could have her whenever he wanted) and we made tentative plans for the following Wednesday. I was hoping like hell that Cyndi would confess everything to me before then because I dearly wanted to participate. Jacking off in the closet wasn't nearly as fulfilling as Cyndi's pussy, not by a long shot.

I gave Cyndi enough of a head start so that she could get home and clean up before I got there. I had taken out a subscription to PHL and was having it delivered to my office and the current issue had arrived the day before, but I hadn't opened it in anticipation of the day's activities. Cyndi was in the kitchen when I got home.

"Oh there you are," she said, "I expected you to be here when I got home."

I kissed her and even though I'm sure she brushed her teeth when she showered, I thought I could taste the faintest trace of someone else's cum. "Had to stop and pick up the latest issue of my magazine," I said.

"Honestly, Rob, I don't know what you see in that stupid magazine."

I grinned, "It's the only way I can feed my fantasy since I can't get you to do it."

"You are disgusting" she said, "I can't believe you would even think of asking me to have sex with another man. I'm your wife, not some round-heeled tramp."

Not ready to give up, I said, "Baby, you are the sexiest and most sexual woman I have ever known and I know you would love it if you would just try."

"Forget it!" she said with a tone of finality in her voice.

That night I couldn't get enough of her. Every time I'd cum, the image of her in Jerry's bed would get me rock hard again. We made love four times that night and Cyndi couldn't get over it.

"Maybe that stupid magazine has its uses after all."

***

On the following Monday, Jerry came to me with a problem.

"Ray called me to his office this morning. He wants copies of the photos."

"Why?" I wanted to know.

"Well, he didn't say and I didn't ask, but we both know the rumors about him using his wife to keep his good customers happy. If I were a betting man, I'd bet he might want to try and blackmail Cyndi into doing the same thing. What should I do?"

I sat there silent and thought about the possibilities. Jerry was between a rock and a hard place - saying no to the boss was not a good career move, but the only reason he still had the photos was so I could be part of the scene, even if only from the closet. In the end, I decided to be bold.

I was waiting for Ray when he came into work the next morning. I told him that I had a personal problem I needed to discuss with him and he led me into his office. What I did was a gamble, but I felt I had solid ground under me so I took the copy of PHL out of my briefcase and handed it to him. Then I took a deep breath and said:

"Turn to page seventy-six" and then waited while he did. "Are you familiar with the magazine?" I asked.

Ray laughed, "Hell yes! I have a subscription."

I forged on, "Then you are familiar with the section on wife-watching?" He nodded yes and I dove in, "I'm one of those husbands who likes to watch. In fact, I was in the closet watching the other night when you and all the boys broke Cyndi's gangbang cherry."

I explained about my situation and how we were using the pictures that Jerry took to manipulate Cyndi into situations where I could watch without her or anyone else knowing.

"Jerry tells me you want a copy of the pictures and I want to know why."

Ray got a big grin on his face and said, "I knew you were my kind of guy. I've been watching Lois for years, only she knows about it. You don't know it, but Lois has been closing deals for me for years now. She loves the variety and the excitement and so do I. I wanted a copy of those pictures so I could blackmail Cyndi into doing the same thing."

I grinned back at him, "Then we have the makings of a deal here. If Cyndi caves in to you, and I'm sure she will, I want to be able to watch whenever possible and I want her exposed to the arrangement you have with Lois. Maybe if Lois talks with her she will be able to convince Cyndi that she should do the same for me. And as a sort of trade of favors, maybe I could use Lois to close a few of my deals."

Ray stood up and stuck out his hand, "Done!" he said.

***

It has been two weeks now since I gave Jerry the go ahead to give Ray a copy of the pictures. Cyndi has had a busy time of it since that day. Ray got the photos on Tuesday and that afternoon, he stopped by the house to talk with Cyndi. I wasn't able to watch that day but Ray filled me in later. He and Cyndi had rolled around on the bed for three hours and when he left, he had Cyndi lined up with her first client for Thursday.

The Wednesday gangbang had the usual guys there and it had started at noon because everyone wanted to fuck Cyndi at least three times that day. The gangbang took place at Jerry's again and again I was in the closet. This time, Cyndi was not at all hesitant when she entered the room and she was an active participant from the word go.

I know it sounds strange, but watching her in action, I was proud of her. For almost four hours, she drained every cock that managed to get hard. Everybody had her three times and two guys actually managed to nail her four times. It was Ray who broke things up by saying that she had to hurry up and beat me home or it was likely she would have stayed there and fucked them all night.

***

The company maintained an apartment in a high-rise on the other side of town; and seven o'clock found me in a hidey-hole that Ray had constructed. The closet had a false wall that hid a small room that was just behind a two-way mirror and I was sitting behind it when a distinguished looking older gentleman ushered Cyndi into the room. She had told me she was having a working dinner with a client that evening, but she of course failed to mention that it wasn't one of her clients. The night was tame compared to the gangbangs, but I still enjoyed watching every minute of it. Cyndi was very active and I was surprised that the older man was able to keep up with her. If her performance and his enjoyment of it were any indication, Ray had just closed another deal.

Cyndi took a shower and cleaned herself up before she left and I had to drive like a mad man to beat her home. I was sitting up in bed when she came into the bedroom and I made the comment:

"My, don't you look good enough to eat."

Cyndi smiled at me and said, "I think I'll take you up on that," and she started undressing. This was something new - she was going to let me eat her pussy right after having fucked someone else and she had never done that before. Was she starting to loosen up? Was I getting closer to having my fantasy realized? Well, if it was going to happen it wasn't going to be that night. I know she had showered and cleaned herself out, but was she sure I wouldn't taste just a little bit of something strange? Or was she hoping I would and not know it? Was this something that she wanted to put over on me? I don't guess I'll ever know the answer to that one, but I do know this - as long as she continues to hide what she's doing from me, I will continue to set her up and be there to watch.

CHAPTER 3

Things started to get very lively for Cyndi and she was being kept very busy by the sexual commitments she had allowed herself to be blackmailed into. There was the usual Wednesday afternoon gangbang, Jerry was seeing her two or three times a week, Ray about the same plus setting her up with clients two or three times a week.

You might have expected that my sex life would suffer because of all she was getting on the side, but I was still getting all I could handle and then some. It seemed that the more Cyndi got, the more she wanted me. A shrink would probably say it was a guilt thing; the more she fucked around on me, the guiltier she felt and the guiltier she felt the more she needed to assuage her guilt by making it up to me. I had a much simpler explanation - the more she got fucked, the more she wanted to get fucked.

However you wanted to look at it one thing was always there - I wasn't any closer to being able to participate.

***

Jerry came to see me at work one day with what he thought was a problem. There were only three guys we worked with who hadn't sampled Cyndi's pussy. Guys being guys, it was inevitable that the three would find out what was going on and once they did, it was equally inevitable that one, two or all three would want to get in on it. That's just what happened and Jerry wanted to know what he should do about it. I gave it moments thought and then asked him if there was any good reason for excluding any of the three. Jerry said none that he could think of so I told him to let them join in.

Simple math said nine guys into one girl twice each did not equal three hours, so on Wednesday morning, I told Cyndi that I had to have dinner with a client that night and not to expect me home before nine. I thought I saw something flicker in her eyes and I would bet that it was the pleasure of knowing that she wouldn't have to cut short her afternoon to hurry home.

That night, I watched from the closet as Cyndi reduced nine guys into exhausted wrecks. It was quarter to eight and she still had half an hour before she had to leave and there wasn't a stiff dick in the house (except mine) and she was pissed.

"Bunch of fucking wimps" she muttered as she got dressed.

As soon as she was gone, Jerry hustled everyone out so that I could come out of the closet. Jerry looked at me and said:

"I don't know where she gets it. She must feed off our energy."

"Yeah, well feel sorry for me, buddy. She'll be waiting for me when I get home and she will expect me to fill whatever void that you guys didn't."

Jerry laughed at me. "You got nobody to blame but yourself. You created the monster, now go home and live with it."

Cyndi was waiting for me when I got home. She was in bed, dressed in what she called her "Fuck me" clothes, high heels, garter belt and nylons. She smiled when I came into the room and opened her arms:

"I haven't thought of anything all day but fucking you. Get over here, baby."

***

I have a theory, but no scientific way of proving it. I think Cyndi's stamina at gangbangs is a function of use. Before I started setting her up, we would make love, peak together and then relax in each other's arms until I was able to get it up again and then we would repeat the cycle. During a gangbang, as soon as one cock pulled out of her another would take its place and so she never came down from her peak. She would just continue on until she ran out of sufficient lubrication and started to feel discomfort. Like I said, I can't prove my theory because there is no way my cock will ever stay hard that long.

Recently, Cyndi has been having me eat her pussy after someone else has fucked her. She has always showered and douched herself first, but I have to wonder why she is having me do it. Is she hoping that I'll get a taste of something strange and call her on it, or does she feel the need to rub my nose in it (so to speak) knowing that she is doing what I have wanted her to do all along and that I know nothing about it.

The only thing I know for sure is that I didn't seem to be any closer to being a participant and the longer it went on, the more desperate I was to play an active part in it. What I was afraid of is that if I let her know that I knew she would stop, in which case I would be farther ahead to stay in the closet and watch.

Do I sound confused? Well, I was, and so I decided on staying with the 'bird in the hand' theory and settle for what I had. Which is why I found myself in the hidey-hole at the company apartment the night that Ray had Cyndi and Lois entertaining some out of town buyers.

This would be the first time that Cyndi and Lois had worked together and apparently, Ray hadn't told Cyndi that Lois would be there because I could see the surprise when she let herself in the apartment and saw Lois. Lois noticed it too:

"No honey, there's no mix-up. We are both supposed to be here. There are five of them and while Ray knows you can handle that many, he didn't want the waiting period to be too long."

Cyndi looked confused and Lois picked up on that too, "Honey, I've been fucking Ray's friends and customers for years. Sometimes he watches and sometimes he doesn't. He tells me that Rob doesn't know what you're doing, is that right?"

Cyndi nodded a yes and Lois said, "That's too bad, you are missing out on a real good thing. There isn't anything better than knowing that you have your husband's permission to scratch your itch whenever you want to and with whomever you want."

Just then there was a knock on the door and suddenly the women were too busy to talk. I had never seen Lois naked before and I was surprised at her tight little body. I wondered why she always kept it hidden under loose 'old lady' style clothes. I was also surprised at her behavior - the woman was a fucking nymphomaniac. I spent four hours behind that two-way watching those five guys try to keep up with the two women. I saw my first triple penetration when Lois took a dick in all three holes. She shook like she was impaled on electric cattle prods and I blew my nuts all over the wall in front of me.

One of the guys tried to use Cyndi's ass and she firmly, but politely declined. When the men were gone Lois said:

"I wish there had been a couple more guys, I've still got the itch. How about you?" she asked Cyndi.

Cyndi looked at her watch and said, "A couple of more would have been nice. I've still got an hour before I have to leave. I thought it would take longer than it did."

Lois smiled and said, "You are in luck, honey, because little Lois always comes prepared" and she picked up the phone and placed a call.

"Barry? Hurry up, baby, I need it."

She hung up the phone and said, "I always want more than Ray's customers can give me so I have a couple of friends waiting in the lounge across the street. I'll share, but I do hope you aren't a racist."

Cyndi gave her a confused look and Lois said, "You'll see."

About a minute later, there was a knock on the door and when Lois opened the door, three very black dudes came in and immediately started undressing. And in less time than it took to write that paragraph, both girls were on their backs with cocks buried in them. The sight of those black bodies on top of and driving into the two white women made my cock as hard as a bar of iron. I watched all three men fuck Cyndi and twice I watched her wrap her red lips around a black cock and suck it to completion. I blew another load against the wall in front of me when I saw the cum leaking out of her mouth and running down her chin.

One of the guys was just getting ready to stick his cock in Cyndi for the third time when Lois said:

"Better check your watch, honey. I think it's time for you to get out of here."

Cyndi looked at her watch and said, "Oh shit!" and she pulled away from the guy trying to mount her and started to grab her clothes. She dressed hurriedly and then stopped on her way to the door to kiss the guy she had just pulled away from:

"Next time, baby, I'll make it up to you." She kissed him again and left.

Obviously Cyndi wasn't a racist, not if she planned on doing it again. Back on the bed, all three men were doing a triple penetration on Lois and despite my already having cum three times, the sight had me hard again in no time. I began to worry though, because I needed to get out of there and get home, but I couldn't leave while Lois and her black studs were still at it. Fortunately, the triple bout seemed to be enough for Lois and as soon as all three of the men had cum, she told them she had to be getting home. As they were leaving one of the guys said:

"Try and bring that other one with you next time. She was really hot."

Lois laughed and said, "I'll see to it that you get all of her that you want."

When the guys were gone, Lois came over to the mirror and put on her lipstick and then she said:

"I'm putting on fresh just for you, Rob. Come on out here and let me suck your cock."

Damn! Ray didn't tell me that he was going to tell Lois that I would be in the closet. I sat there frozen, not knowing what to do. The plan never included me being unfaithful to Cyndi and it was something that I hadn't even considered. Lois decided that I wasn't moving fast enough and she came after me. The sliding panel slid open and she looked in at me trying to stuff a hard-on back into my pants:

"You are wasting your time, lover. I'm not letting you out of this apartment until I suck your cock or you fuck me." Then she noticed the mess on the wall in front of me, "Oh poor, baby, did we turn you on? Do you have any left for me?"

She led me out of the closet, undressed me, and then gave me the most erotic fuck of my life. It wasn't that she was better in bed than Cyndi, she just pushed all the right buttons.

"Did you like seeing your white wife sucking those big, black cocks? How does it feel knowing that your cock is soaking in the cum of eight different men? You just kissed me and I've had the cum of four men in my mouth tonight. Could you taste it? Did you like it? Do you like fucking your wife after she has had nine guys dumping their loads in her for four hours?"

And on and on like that for an hour and a half. If I had a button that could be pushed, Lois found it and pushed it. Every time I knew that I was done, Lois would say something like, "Would you like to see Cyndi do an all-black gangbang? Black cocks shooting cum into every hole, wouldn't you like that?" and I'd be hard again.

God, what a night. I'd never been so thoroughly drained in all my life. When I got home, Cyndi was waiting in her 'fuck me' clothes and for the first time in our married life, I told her I was too tired and I went to bed.

***

The next day, I decided that I needed some time off to think about things, so I called Vegas and made reservations at a hotel and arranged for tee times on Thursday and Friday. Then I told Jerry that I was going to tell Cyndi that I had to go out of town on business for two days. Then I told Ray that I was taking a couple of vacation days and he laughed and said:

"Yeah, Lois can do that to a guy sometimes."

I spent two days playing golf, watching some of the lounge shows and contemplating my future with Cyndi. Not that I meant I was going to break up with her or anything like that, but I was going to have to do something about our sex life. I still had hopes that she would admit to things and allow me in, but if I had to I was going to force the issue by 'catching her in the act" or by confronting her with, "So and so told me that you - fill in the blank -" and take it from there.

I came home Friday evening to an empty house and on a hunch, I checked the medicine cabinet and her diaphragm wasn't there. I wondered who was getting lucky, Jerry, Ray, Ray's customers or had Lois set her up with an all-black gang fuck? I was sitting in bed reading when she came home at one in the morning. She was surprised to see me and said:

"I didn't expect you until tomorrow morning."

I told her the meeting ended early and I had caught an early flight. I didn't ask her where she'd been and she didn't volunteer to tell me, but when I got out of bed and started undressing, her she got real nervous.

"Let me take a shower first" she said, "I smell of cigarette smoke."

"No" I said as I pushed her back on the bed, "I haven't thought of anything since I left. I let you down the other night and now I've got three days of need stored up. I want you now, just the way you are" and I pushed her back on the bed.

I lowered my face to her pussy and she tried to push me away, "No baby, please let me shower" but I was not going to be denied. I didn't even need to taste her pussy to know that she had been freshly fucked, her pussy hairs had dried cum all over them.

As soon as my tongue touched her, the knowledge that for the first time I was going to taste another man's (or men's) cum in her pussy made my cock tingle. I felt her body tense up, waiting for me to say something.

"Damn! You must have been thinking about me coming home as much as I thought about getting home. It sure got you wet." And then I gave a little laugh and said in a joking tone, "Either that or you just left your lover." At that she pushed her pussy in my face, gave a low moan and said:

"Yes baby, that's it. I just left my lover and that wetness is his cum. Suck it out of me, baby, suck his cum out of me before you fuck me."

"God, but I really wish that you meant that" I said, treating it as a joke while all the time knowing that it was true. After several minutes of eating her pussy, I climbed on top of my wife and for the first time fucked my wife while she still had the cum of someone else in her. We both climaxed about the same time, but my cock didn't go soft like it usually did. I stayed hard and I kept fucking her until I came a second time.

"What got into you?" she wanted to know.

"Just the thought of fucking you right after someone else."

"Honestly, Rob, aren't you ever going to get over that foolishness?"

***

I called Jerry the next day and he filled me in on what had happened while I was gone. He swung by the house at noon on Thursday and caught Cyndi at home. The two of them had spent the afternoon in bed, gone out to dinner, and then they had gone back to our place and Cyndi had fucked Jerry until he couldn't get it up any more and then Jerry had spent the night. They had fucked a couple of times the next morning, gone out for lunch and then had spent the afternoon in bed. When Jerry suggested that they go out for dinner, Cyndi had said sorry, but she had a previous engagement. I had no idea who I followed into her pussy Friday night.

Monday, I stopped by Ray's office and asked him when the next time would be that he would have Lois and Cyndi together.

"It looks like this Thursday, why?"

"Because I'm going to ask Lois for a favor."

Ray laughed and said, "Just as long as you are aware that she'll make you pay for it."

I went to my office and called Lois, asked her for a favor and when she said she would do it, I told her what I wanted. Monday was a slow day for Cyndi; she only got fucked by me. Tuesday she had Jerry in the afternoon and me at bedtime. Wednesday was the weekly gangbang, but it was Thursday that I was waiting for. I was in the closet when Cyndi came in and Lois arrived about five minutes later. There was a bunch of small talk and then Lois said:

"Are you ever going to tell Rob what you are doing?"

Cyndi said no, that she never intended that I should find out. Lois said:

"That's not what I asked you. I asked you if you were ever going to tell him. As far as his finding out, I'm pretty sure he already knows."

Cyndi got a frown on her face and asked, "Why do you say that?"

Lois gave a little chuckle and said, "Because, honey, you have been fucked by every man that Rob works with and guys talk. Sooner or later the talk will get to Rob and I'm pretty sure from some of the things I've heard that it already has."

Cyndi frowned again, "That couldn't be. He would have said something to me by now."

Lois said, "Not if he doesn't want to upset the marriage. He is probably waiting for you to confess. He probably knows that things could get nasty if he confronts you on it. Remember, honey, you may be doing something he wants you to do, but you are still doing it behind his back and that's called cheating."

Cyndi was quiet for a moment and then she said, "How can I find out for sure?"

Lois laughed, "That one's easy, honey. When you go home tonight, don't shower or douche and get Rob to go down on you. He's not stupid. You will have the cum of at least six guys in you and if Rob eats you but says nothing except for making some stupid remark about how wet you are, you'll know."

I saw the look on Cyndi's face and I knew she was remembering last Friday night. Lois went on:

"Let me tell you, honey, if you want your marriage to survive, you need to get Rob involved before it becomes set in his mind that you are a lying, cheating bitch."

Just then, there was a knock on the door and the evening's entertainment began. There were seven guys and I recognized most of them as very good customers of the firm. For the next four hours, I watched them play with the ladies and wished that I could be out there with them. By my count, Cyndi had cum eleven times, not counting what went down her throat, and it would be interesting to see if she followed Lois's advice and didn't clean up before I got to her. If she didn't, I was one step closer to having everything out in the open. Just before Cyndi left, Lois said:

"My black friends were quite taken with you the other night and they want to know if you would like to get together with them again."

Cyndi smiled and said, "Sure, why not. Set it up and let me know when."

The door hadn't completely closed behind Cyndi and I was out of the closet and on my way out of the apartment. It was obvious that Lois was expecting me to stay and play, but I rushed past her and said:

"I'll call you tomorrow. Wish me luck."

I would have to drive like hell to beat Cyndi home and I wanted to be there when she walked in. She came into the bedroom and I pulled down the covers to display my hard-on and said:

"I've been waiting for you, baby."

She smiled and began undressing. "I feel like a little sixty-nine tonight," she said as she walked over to the bed and swung around over me. I could see drops of cum, still wet, on her pussy lips as her cunt came down toward my face. I felt her lips take in my cock as I buried my face in her cunt.

CHAPTER 4

It was the first time that I'd eaten Cyndi's pussy with a full load (or loads) of cum in her and it turned me on more than I would have believed possible. I licked and sucked for a good five minutes before I pulled away from her and said:

"Damn baby, you are really wet tonight. You must have been thinking all day about coming home and screwing my brains out."

Cyndi didn't say anything, she just swung around and lowered herself on my upright pole. She stared down into my face as she rode me, but I couldn't read her expression. I was betting that she now had a pretty good idea that I knew something, but she probably wasn't quite sure what. Did I know it all, or just some of it, and I wondered what her next move would be. After a rather strenuous bout, we fell asleep in each other's arms.

I woke up in the morning and went downstairs where I found Cyndi sipping coffee and reading my latest issue of Penthouse Letters. I was all set to say something, but at the last second I decided to keep my mouth shut and see where things would go. I poured a cup of coffee and sat down at the table.

"Good morning, lover" she said, "Got time for a quickie before you go to work?"

I wondered why, if she wanted a quickie, she hadn't just waked me up with a blowjob or by playing with my dick, but then I thought that maybe she was reading something in the magazine that made her horny. Whatever, I said I would love an early morning fuck and we went back to bed.

Later, while she was in the shower, I went back down stairs and picked up the magazine and saw that it was turned to "Cluster Fucks" and the letter on the page had the heading, "He Loved It when His Wife Disappeared In An Ocean Of Black Bodies." As I read the title, I remembered her saying "next time baby, I'll make it up to you" when she and Lois were doing the black guys. And when Lois had asked her if she wanted to get together with them again she had said, "Why not? Set it up."

Was it possible that Cyndi was coming up with her own sexual hang-up, fucking blacks, and that maybe she could now understand my having a sexual hang-up too?

It was Wednesday, Cyndi's regular gangbang day with Jerry and all the guys and all morning when the phone rang, I grabbed it hoping to hear Cyndi say, "Guess what, lover? Today is your lucky day, "but it didn't happen. At eleven-thirty, I called her and told her I would be working late again and then I told my secretary that I had to go see a client.

On the drive to Jerry's, I again contemplated just going ahead and confronting Cyndi, but again I decided not to. If I brought it up, it would be like I was confronting her on cheating on me, which she was, but I was afraid of what it might do to us and our marriage. I loved the slut and didn't want to do anything that might jeopardize our marriage, even if it meant more years of me hiding in the closet. I felt that it had to come from her, but that didn't mean that I couldn't try to nudge or help move her in that direction.

***

Tuesday, I had called Lois and asked her to make sure that the deal she was setting up with her black friends would take place in the company apartment and not to forget to let me know when. She gave me her throaty laugh and said:

"You do love to see those black poles go into her white hole, don't you?"

I gave her back a laugh and told her that she had it all wrong, "I got off on seeing you take on three at once."

She giggled, "I guess I'll have to do it again, just for you."

Then I asked her to keep working on Cyndi to tell me what was going on. I was in the closet when Cyndi came into the bedroom:

"Good news, guys. I don't have to leave early today. So, I need a cock to suck and somebody to fuck me. Who's first?"

For five hours I watched and stroked myself as the wanton slut that I was married to destroyed seven guys. Each one fucked her twice and four managed to get it up three times, but only Jerry was able to get it hard a fourth time. She sucked cocks, gave hand jobs, did everything she could think of to get them up again, but couldn't do it. The guys started leaving and soon it was just Cyndi and Jerry. She was lying next to him on the bed and trying to get him up for a fifth time and she said:

"How well do you know, Rob?"

Jerry said that he thought he knew me pretty well and Cyndi said, "His fantasy has always been for me to do what I'm doing right now. How do you think he would react if I told him that I was?"

Jerry was quiet for a bit and then he said, "He would probably be pissed at first, not because of what you are doing, but because you have been keeping it from him. He will stay pissed until you tell him when you are going to do it again and tell him that you want him to be there."

Cyndi gave him a thoughtful look; "Do you really think so?"

And Jerry said, "I think I could safely bet the farm on it."

She scooted down on the bed and took his cock in her mouth and damned if she didn't manage to get him hard again.

Cyndi was sitting on the bed reading when I got home. "Rough day?" she asked.

"Parts of it were hard, but I think I see success in the future for something I'm working on."

She smiled and said, "Too tired to eat my pussy and then fuck me a couple of times?"

I said, "I'm always willing to give it a shot. What's going on with you lately? It seems like your pussy is always wet. If I didn't know better I'd think you had a half a dozen lovers on the side."

I felt her body tense, but she relaxed when my tongue parted her pussy lips. How do you explain what it feels like to suck the accumulated cum of seven guys out of your wife and then follow them into her pussy? I can't! It's a feeling like no other I have ever felt and the only thing I do know for sure is that I'll never get tired of doing it. We made love twice that night before falling asleep in each other's arms and she woke me up with a blowjob the next morning.

***

I hadn't been in my office five minutes when Lois called me, "I just got off the phone with your black cock-loving whore of a wife (God, but she did know how to push my buttons) and we are all set for two this afternoon. Going to be there?"

"Try and keep me away," I said.

Lois was already in the apartment when I got there, "I thought I'd get here early and suck your cock. That way you won't make such a mess on the wall as you watch those hard black cocks being stuffed into your lily white wife's mouth and pussy."

"Why do you talk that way?" I asked, "I've watched you and you are as big a slut for black cock as anyone I've ever seen."

She laughed, "I know, baby" she said as she fished my cock out, "but I'm not yours and she is."

She took my stiff cock and led me to the hiding place in the closet, "We don't want the black cock-loving slut to walk in on us, now do we?"

It did not take her long to get me off; the picture of Cyndi's lips wrapped around a black dick had me so hot that I exploded into Lois's mouth in less than two minutes.

"My, my, kind of excited are we? I won't bother tucking it back in because I know you'll have it out again as soon as those hard black cocks begin penetrating the whore you are married to."

About ten minutes later, guys started to arrive and by the time Cyndi got there, there were ten naked black studs waiting for her. I don't know why black on white is so erotic, but my cock stayed hard the whole time that the two women serviced the black crowd. I wished I had a camera or a camcorder because everything I saw was a turn-on.

Cyndi on hands and knees with a cock in her mouth and one fucking her from behind. Lois doing three at a time. Cyndi sitting on one cock while sucking another and Cyndi with a cock in each hand and one in her mouth as another guy tried to mount her from behind.

I watched Cyndi take cock after cock and I thought back to the letter that she had been reading in PHL and I wondered again if fucking blacks was her thing like watching was mine. I got a partial answer a moment later when one of the guys said he wanted to fuck her in her ass. She immediately turned over and got on her hands and knees - so much for keeping something just for Rob. She squealed with pleasure while the guy fucked her butt, so much so that a couple of other guys wanted to fuck her there too. For the next half hour, Cyndi was on her knees, head buried in a pillow, as one after another the other guys fucked her ass.

I had been doing my best not to beat my meat while watching, wanting to save it for Cyndi when we got home, but I started whacking off in earnest when one of the guys pulled Cyndi up and two other guys joined him and they gave her first triple penetration. When I saw those three hard black cocks pushing into her little white body, I lost it and blew a load all over the wall in front of me.

Then Lois (for my benefit no doubt) started directing things. She got everyone organized so that Cyndi had a cock in her mouth, a cock in her pussy, a cock in her ass and a cock in each hand. It was not only mind blowing, but I blew a second load onto the wall. Things started winding down after that as one after another the guys got dressed and left. Soon it was just Cyndi, Lois, and a guy that I recognized as the guy Cyndi had told she'd make it up to the next time.

Then Lois dressed and as she got ready to leave she said, "I'll get out of here and leave you two love birds alone" and as she said it she was looking right at the mirror where she knew I was and I knew that she was trying to tell me something.

As soon as she was gone, Cyndi and the man still there started kissing and they kept it up for several minutes. When they broke apart the man said:

"Baby, you sure are something else."

Cyndi, who had never stopped stroking his cock, said, "You aren't too bad yourself. I love the way you fuck me. You sure you don't mind sharing me with your buddies?"

He laughed and said, "If they didn't take the edge off of you, I couldn't keep up. When can I see you again?"

Cyndi said, "I don't know, lover. It was easy last Friday because my husband was out of town. Don't worry. I'll think of something."

I suddenly knew what Lois had been telling me - Cyndi now had a boyfriend! It was a sobering thought and one that meant I needed to bring things to a head, and soon.

***

Cyndi was waiting for me when I got home. She was sitting up in bed and reading PHL when I came in and when I saw it I said:

"I thought you didn't like that rag."

She put it down and said, "I'm still trying to get some insight into why you want your wife to be a whore while you watch."

I undressed and my erection jumped out and stood there quivering and I said, "See him jutting out and eager to be buried in your pussy? He is rock hard because I spent the last six hours at work imagining you in a room full of black men who took turns fucking you right up to the moment where you said, 'Sorry, fellows, I have to stop now and hurry home to my husband.' Imagine how hard he would be if he was around for the real thing?"

She gave me an odd look, "Really? You imagined me fucking black men? Why?"

I laughed, "Because, my love, I've seen the letters that you have been reading in that magazine. They all are about white housewives being fucked by black men. I think you have a fantasy of your own now - being fucked by black men."

She gave me another odd look, "You think seeing me fuck a black man would turn you on?"

I said, "Absolutely" and buried my face in her pussy. It was too clean so I knew she had cleaned up when she got home.

"Would you eat me after I fucked this black man? Would you suck my pussy after he had sprayed me full of his cum?"

I pulled away from her cunt long enough to say, "In a heartbeat, sweetie, in a heartbeat."

"Would you fuck me after he did?" I nodded a yes.

"And you wouldn't get jealous or leave me?" Again I nodded a yes. "I don't think I can believe that" she said.

"I'll prove it to you," I said.

"How?" she wanted to know.

I smiled and said, "I'll furnish the black man."

I don't know which of us was the most insatiable that night, but neither of us could leave the other alone. We were both exhausted when we finally fell asleep.

**

The next morning, I called Lois as soon as I got to the office. "Can you arrange a meeting between me and the guy who was still there with Cyndi when you left?" She asked why and I explained my plan to her.

"His name is Hank" she said, "and I'm pretty sure he'll go for it."

I walked into the restaurant at noon and spotted him at a table in the corner. I walked up to the table and stuck out my hand:

"Hank? I'm Rob."

He stood and took my hand and we both sat down. "What's this all about?" he wanted to know, "All Lois would tell me was that you wanted to discuss something with me that would be to our mutual benefit."

I smiled and said, "You could say that" and then I told him who I was and what I wanted and he smiled.

We finished dinner and I asked Cyndi to go put on her "fuck me" clothes while I cleared the table. She giggled and said, "Is my baby horny tonight? Thinking of me with black men again?"

I smiled and said, "Something like that."

Ten minutes later, she came back into the kitchen wearing only high heels and nylons with a garter belt.

"Is your dick hard, sailor?"

I said that it always was where she was concerned and I took her by the hand and led her to the living room where, sitting naked on the sofa with a hard cock jutting up out of his lap, sat Hank.

"You entertain our guest while I finish in the kitchen" and I left her standing there in opened mouth surprise.

I gave them ten minutes and when I came back, they were gone. I headed to the bedroom where I found Cyndi, legs spread wide with her high heels pointing up at the ceiling, moaning:

"Fuck me, baby, fuck me."

Between those spread legs and doing his best to imitate a jack hammer was Hank and he smiled when he saw me.

"It's about time you got here. Put something in her mouth and shut her up."

I walked over to the bed and pushed my hard cock against Cyndi's lips. She opened her eyes and looked at me and I smiled at her and said:

"Proof enough?"

Hank and I took turns fucking Cyndi damn near all night. When he finally staggered out the door at four in the morning, I got down and buried my face in Cyndi's pussy and started licking at the mess that Hank and I had made. Cyndi's hands dug into my hair and she pulled me tight into her cunt:

"You miserable, bastard! You've known! You've known all along that your wife is a slut and a whore."

I didn't say a thing, I just kept on eating her pussy until she had an orgasm and then I crawled up next to her and took her in my arms:

"Believe me now?"

"How long have you known?"

She had tears on her cheeks and I wiped them away and said, "Go to sleep. We can talk about it in the morning."

***

The next day, I told her most of it. I did not tell her how Jerry and I had set her up that first time, but I did tell her that I came back from the beer run and found out what was happening. I told her that I had backed out of the room before anyone had noticed me and then kept peeking in. I told her that I caught Jerry when he came out of the room and told him I wouldn't put a stop to things if he would take the pictures. I told her that when she hadn't confessed all the next morning that Jerry and I had used to photos to set her up and that I had been watching ever since. I told her about my deal with Roy and about the hidden room in the closet. And I told her about making the decision to wait until she brought things out into the open on her own until I saw her with Hank and how she seem to be developing a relationship with him.

"When I saw what was happening between you two, I knew I had to come out of the closet before I lost you to another man."

She reached out and touched my cheek, "Oh baby, I'm sorry you thought that. I do like him and I love fucking him, but I don't love him. You are not going to lose me to anybody else - ever. I love you too much to ever leave you. And I love you too much to ever hurt you, which is why I kept everything from you. I just couldn't believe you would keep me if you found out what a whore I'd become.

"I knew I was doing what you said you wanted me to do, but when I would come home from doing what I'd just done I'd look back on it and I just couldn't believe that you would accept it. I didn't want to take a chance on losing you so I kept quiet."

I smiled at her, "Well, the cat's out of the bag now, sweetie, and we both know you are a slut and a whore for cock, both black and white. You going to keep on going?"

She threw herself in my arms and said, "Oh God yes. And right now your whore wants your cock. Fuck going to work today, let's go to bed.

***

That was a year ago. Cyndi still has her regular Wednesday gangbang only now I am a part of it. It was a little awkward for the guys at first, but what the hell - fuck them, right? I mean they all thought they were fucking my wife behind my back so a little discomfort is the least they should suffer. The way we did it was she and Jerry moved the gangbang to our house because Jerry was having his place painted and then I walked in on them and "caught them in the act." The looks on the faces were priceless and even more so when I undressed and joined them.

Cyndi still fucks Ray's customers and clients and I have even used her to keep some of mine happy. She and Lois still do a black gangbang every two weeks or so and I have to hide in the closet for that. She even brought Lois home with her one night and the two of them destroyed me.

The most interesting development is that Cyndi now has a steady boyfriend, two of them if you count Jerry. She and Hank go out on a regular basis and he occasionally takes her to a party where she ends up taking on all comers. She comes home and tells me about it and we fuck like newlyweds.

My favorite story is the one where hank took her to his brother's birthday party and it turned into a massive gangbang. They threw four mattresses down on the living room floor and Cyndi and three other girls lay down and took on thirty-seven guys. Cyndi is quite proud of the fact that by the end of the party, she was still going strong while the other girls had quit.

Another development is the rivalry that has occurred between Jerry and Hank. Whenever I had to leave on business, there was always a tug of war between the two as to which one Cyndi would spend her time with. It took a while but Cyndi finally resolved the issue by saying she wouldn't stay with either of them. She stays home and they both stay with her. As for me, I walk around with a constant hard-on and wonder what is going to happen next.

The End

Here is a sample from another story you may enjoy:

MORE THAN
She Can Take

EROTICA SHORT STORIES, **VOL.28**

JUST PLAIN BOB

I never did tell Lois that she had been busted. I just accepted the fact that she was an unfaithful whore and let it go. I had no idea how long it had been going on and no idea why. I had thought that we had a good marriage and I know, or at least I thought I did, that there was nothing wrong with our sex life. We made love three and sometimes four times a week, sometimes twice in a night and I was willing to do anything that she wanted. What was important, however, is that the marriage was dead – not over, just dead.

Why not over? Because I didn't have the energy for it. I'd been married once before and my first divorce had ruined me financially and had made me into an emotional basket case for years. If I was thirty-five or forty, I might have done it, but not at fifty. Why start over? Lois kept a clean house, was a good cook, and did the laundry and all the other things that a wife does to make life move smoothly. We didn't argue or fight so I just decided to settle for a comfortable existence. So I said nothing about what I saw and life went on.

The only change was that I stopped having sex with Lois. When she asked why, I told her that I was having some problems and was seeing a doctor. After two months, I told her that I had acute erectile dysfunction and that I couldn't get a hard on. Another two months went by and then I told her that I had tried everything that the doctor had suggested, but that nothing worked and she would just have to get used to the fact that the sexual part of our marriage was over. She wasn't really happy about it, but I really didn't give a shit about how she felt about it.

I didn't give up sex though. There was a woman I went to high school with and she had lost her husband in the First Gulf War and she supplemented her income by servicing a few select customers and I paid her a visit twice a week.

***

Lois and I were in the habit of going out for breakfast every

Saturday and Sunday and we always ate at the same restaurant. The place was just around the corner from where I worked and I had lunch in there two or three times during the week. There was a waitress working there named Tiffany and she was a lot of fun to be around. A tall girl, almost six feet, and with a hard, tight body to die for. She had the goods and she knew how to dress to show them off. Low hip-huggers and tops that emphasized her high breasts and flat stomach. She had a wild side to her and she had several tattoos and a piercing or two that she also loved to show off.

I got in the habit of flirting with her at lunchtime and after a couple of months, we had developed a rapport. The flirting progressed from the simple to the borderline raunchy and Tiff gave as good as she got. She had a stud through her tongue and one day I said, "One of these days you are going to have to explain or better yet, show me what the purpose of that thing is."

She stuck her tongue out at me and said, "First you will have to show me that your health insurance is up to date. When I put you in the hospital I want to know that you'll be taken care of."

One day when I came in after not stopping in for a week, she came up to my table and lifted her top to show me that she'd had her navel pierced and was sporting what looked like a diamond stick pin.

"You know, Tiff, I have a barely controllable urge to kiss your belly."

If you enjoyed this sample then look for More Than She Can Take.

Also by this Author:

The Prodigal Family: The Abbotts

Watching My Shared Wife

The Waitress and the Runaway Husband

Baiting Mr. Little

Too Hot for Henry

Chuck's Fantasy

The Redhead's Desires

Rescued at Riley's

His Every Fantasy

Open Mike Night

Pursuit for Revenge

Why Does He Do That?

Halloween & Drugs

Tracey

When Rob Met Kari

Becoming a Shared Wife, Vol. 1 –
(Wife Sharing and Other Adventures)

Becoming a Shared Wife, Vol. 2 –
(Hazardous Wives)

Becoming a Shared Wife, Vol. 3 –
(Wives Who Stray)

Dirty Love

Hot & Tight

Her Illicit Adventures

What I Want To Do To Her

Too Fun To Give Up

Creamed

Stepping Out

From the Author

WANT FREE COPIES OF MY BOOKS?
Just visit my blog and download free copies of my books:
awesomeauthors.org/justplainbob

Yes, I write about sluts and whores because as everyone knows, you tend to write about the things you know. And I do like sluts and whores, just not the ones that lie to me and cheat on me.

So be forewarned - if you click on a Just Plain Bob story you will be getting sluts, whores and husbands who do not kill, maim and destroy. There are other things you will rarely find in a Just Plain Bob story.

If you enjoyed any of my books then please share the love and promote my books in Amazon. I would really appreciate your honest reviews, too!

Good news is always welcome.

One Last Thing, For Kindle Readers...

When you turn the page, Kindle will give you the opportunity to rate this book and share your thoughts on Facebook and Twitter. If you enjoyed my writings, would you please take a few seconds to let your friends know about it? Because... when they enjoy they will be grateful to you and so will I.

Thank you!

Just Plain Bob
justplainbob@awesomeauthors.org

You may also like the books by these authors:

WIVES
HUSBANDS *and*
LOVERS

A COLLECTION OF NINE SEX STORIES

BEN E. DORM

The audacity of the question caught Barbara by surprise. She blinks and gulps at her drink, then eventually splutters because she forgot it was wine in the glass. Swigging the stuff down like water was a mistake.

Struggling, Barbara stammers, "I... uh... I mean to say, Tuh-Tanya..." The heat rises in her face and she falls silent. Barbara doesn't have the words to respond. Her mouth hangs open while thoughts collide in a discordant jumble of conflicting impressions.

Everything is all furred up by the afternoon wine. *Dear God*, she thought, *it must be a bottle each by now!*

Barbara eyes, an offending article, a bottle of Sauvignon Blanc sat on the low table in front of her. Rather blurry, Barbara shifts on the very large, very comfortable three-seater sofa. She realizes that it's the third bottle, but it registers vaguely.

Slack-faced she lifts her face towards her host when Tanya cajoles her with, "Come on, Babs. Don't be shy. It's just a laugh."

Looking at the younger woman – who seems unaffected by so much drink – Barbara sees mischievous eyes twinkling in Tanya's elfin face. She takes in the detail of Tanya's platinum-blonde bobbed hair, dark roots visible in a central parting which, she believes, are the season's *de-rigueur*. She thinks dark roots are a particularly trampy look, but acknowledges Tanya carries it off well. In Barbara's estimation her host is a very pretty girl, but the understanding is slowly dawning and Barbara is coming to realize the innocence the young woman projects are rather misleading.

Barbara thinks the tramp style might be appropriate as she lowers her appraisal to Tanya's generous bosom beneath the tight, button-fronted blouse and smart, waist-length fawn jacket. A high-hemmed skirt rides up to Tanya's thighs, exposing a lot of bare, gym-toned and pleasantly tanned leg and Barbara is suddenly even more self-conscious when confronted with Tanya's physical appeal.

"Oh, Tanya, I don't know if that's entirely appropriate…" says Barbara, her tone stiff and pompous. She gulps more wine and wonders how the Liverpudlian girl can be so confident and self-assured, envy at Tanya's effervescence mixing in with what she perceives as her own repressed and strait-laced character.

Tanya's eyes roll as she says, "You won't shock me, Babs. I could tell you things I've done…" Then Tanya's glance flicks to Barbara's empty glass. "A top up?" she asks, reaching for the bottle.

"Oh, God, Tanya, I shouldn't. It's only three o'clock…"

But Barbara soon finds herself holding yet another brimming glass while Tanya grins at her.

"So, come on, Barbara," the blonde insists. "Tell me – what's the dirtiest thing you've ever done? Ever been to an orgy?"

Enough is enough, Barbara decides. "Of course not!" she gasps, bristling with indignation. "How absurd!"

Unfazed, Tanya laughs and continues with, "A threeway, then? Ever had two blokes at the same time?" Her expression turns vulpine, pale-blue eyes narrowing to match the sly grin Tanya fixes on Barbara. "A man and another woman?" Tanya adds, sipping wine, attention rapt and fixed on Barbara's face.

Barbara gasps again. "Tanya, please!" Her mouth opens and closes as she struggles with the disconcerting effects of afternoon drinking and the shocking interview. The wine combined with a totally unexpected line of questioning has her struggling for composure. This *isn't* what she's used to at all. "Why do you insist on embarrassing me?" she breathes.

Tanya laughs again before smiling at Barbara, her look contrite.

Holding up a conciliatory hand, Tanya says, "Okay, Babs, I'm sorry. I didn't mean any offense. I'm just a gobby cow. Always have been. I'm only teasin' ya."

It's the girl's accent, her blonde hair, the confidence and her youth that goads Barbara into revealing more than she knows is wise. Despite Tanya being at least fifteen years her junior, Barbara, at just over forty, feels so staid and unworldly – so bloody middle-class and *suburban*. She knows it's unwise but, fuddled with drink and confronted with Tanya's supposed contrition, Barbara feels obliged to blurt her innermost and very intimate fantasies.

"Well," she says, voice low as she avoids Tanya's eyes, "if you must know…"

If you enjoyed this sample then look for <u>**Wives, Husbands, Lovers**</u>.

Amy Redek

THE GOOD
TWELVE

12 STORIES
IN ONE

I was orphaned at an early age and was most fortunate to be taken in by Peter and Mary Withers, for I took the place of the child they never had.

Peter was the gamekeeper for Lord Carlton on his estate in Wiltshire and Mary helped out in the house when they had guests, which was mostly in the shooting season. We lived in the lodge at the entrance to the estate and were about a mile from the small village down the lane.

I was happy there as I grew up and Peter saw to my schooling for there was nowhere else I could go for this. Being the gamekeeper, he knew all about animals and birds that lived out in the woods and fields and when I went out with him, he would point out the different species and how to track them. Though part of his job was to keep the poachers at bay and stop them from snaring the pheasants and grouse.

It was some years before he would take me out with him on his nightly prowls, moving quietly to try and find traps that the poachers would set up in the woods. I got to learn the most likely places they would be set and I was quite pleased when I did find one.

'Well done Tom,' he would cry and ruffle the hair of my head, a habit of his for I was far shorter than he was.

One of the turning points of my life was when I was allowed to go into the pub with him. I'd been refused entry before because I was too small but now that I was growing up, they turned a blind eye to me going in with him as long as I behaved myself.

I used to like those evenings, though it was only twice a week. We'd have our dinner and then we'd set off for the pub in the village which was a good mile down the lane. It was only a small place, but now that I was older, they let me in and it was Old Percy who bought me my first beer. It was only half a pint of bitter, but it made the night for me to drink with the locals.

Peter and I would settle ourselves by the log fire and though I didn't smoke or wouldn't have been allowed to anyway, I did like the smell of his pipe when he lit it. He would stretch out his legs and puff away and I would stretch my feet out too and listen to the older men talk.

Though most of what they talked about went over my head and after drinking my small half pint of beer, I would drowse in front of the fire only catching half of what they said. Peter would have maybe three pints but drew the line with me, saying that half was enough. In spite of this restriction on my drinking, I still enjoyed those evenings.

Come ten o'clock, he would finish his beer and wake me up and tell me it was time for bed and that I couldn't sleep in the pub. We would then walk the mile back home and invariable, Mary would be in bed but she always left us a little something to eat before we went to bed. I think she would have been annoyed if she knew that Peter was letting me drink beer when I was out with him.

If you enjoyed this sample then look for <u>The Good Twelve</u>.

Corrupting the
CHOIR BOY

INTENSE EROTICA

JACK RYDER

It felt embarrassing somehow to still be forced to wear this stupid black and white choir robe. The pastor informed me that the women's committee had insisted I wear it even though I only got up to sing solo during the noon service. That sort of creeped me out that a bunch of old church ladies wanted me to look like some young altar boy to sing a couple of hymns solo.

Margaret was sitting in the front row as she has since her divorce six months ago. She has made it a point to sit as close to me as she can. She has told me that she likes a good view when I'm singing. At first, I thought that she was just flattering me. But as time progressed, she has added little flirtations every week. If I wasn't so much younger, I would swear that she has been hitting on me.

At thirty eight years old, Margaret is still a smokin' hot redhead. She sort of puts me in mind of that "Lady Heather" character in the CSI TV series. Today she is wearing a very tight navy blue skirt. Although it is not exactly a miniskirt, it fits her so tight that I can barely keep my eyes off her gloriously sexy round ass each time we have to stand up.

Although her white blouse is suitable for church wear, it fits so tight that I can easily see the outline of both her 34D breasts. I can almost make out the edges of her areolas. But every time she leans forward, her blazer falls open enough that I get a good gaze at her tits. I find it curious that she has unfastened a couple of more buttons at the top of her blouse just before I'm about to get up to sing.

Pastor Boer was just beginning his weekly church calendar announcements. (Yes…that is really his name. He pronounces it BARE, but you can guess what most of us call him). As he was making a lame joke out of the mistake on the schedule that had been printed as pot-lick rather than potluck, Margaret leaned over just far enough that I could see most of her golden brown jugs. She was not wearing a bra and I could see most of both breasts except for her nipples.

I could feel a wiggle between my legs as I glanced up to find that she could tell where I had been looking. She was smiling as she reached over and gently laid her hand on my thigh. "Your singing always inspires me so deeply," she whispered as her fingers slowly grazed up my inseam. "I enjoy the view as well," she giggled softly. My body vibrated as a finger brushed across my now fully erect prick. "Go...inspire me," She chuckled just as the pastor announced my name.

I was actually really glad that I had the stupid robe on as I walked to the front by the choir loft. The robe would at least conceal the boner throbbing in my pants. I sort of had to slouch forward a bit so the robe would hang forward enough to cover the bulge. "Stand tall, sweetie," Margaret giggled softly as I turned to face the congregation.

Once Larry the organist started playing the anthem I had chosen, my dick went soft as I concentrated on the music. I deftly reached forward and quietly shut off the microphone. With my deep and bellowing baritone voice, I would not need it. I was nearly through the first verse when I made the mistake of glancing over at Margaret. She had a huge goofy grin on her face and her legs were spread wide apart.

The pastor always sits in a folding chair behind the pedestal pulpit while I sing. This way he is not a distraction and it gives him time to go over his sermon notes. It also blocks his view of the congregation. I was the only one in the church that could see that she was not wearing panties. I was the only one that could see her bare bald pussy.

I was so distracted by the muff shot that Margaret was giving me, that I accidently skipped to the 3rd verse of the song completely leaving out the second verse and the refrain in between. My face was as red as a fire truck as I walked back to my seat with the entire congregation looking at me with curiosity. I was also sweating profusely even though it was fairly chilly in the church. "Were you thinking something naughty?" Margaret laughed softly as I sat down.

If you enjoyed this sample then look for **Corrupting The Choirboy**.

Less Than Yesterday

Lilith Jones

Hot Romance Erotica

"We said we wouldn't start a baby until we'd gone for a year without needing my paycheck," she said. It hadn't been a year, had it?

"Well, I wasn't talking about starting anything tonight. It's been more than eleven months. And, if we aren't going to make the goal next month, where is the huge expenditure going to come from? . . . Not to end a sentence with a preposition or anything."

"Ted! That's not really a rule."

"Yes, dear," Ted said, sounding like he thought she was trying to change the subject. He was probably right, too, but he didn't pursue the subject. Ted was, she kept reminding herself, nice.

Thursday, a few weeks later, she started a new disk of pills. That night, with Ted working late, she realized what that meant. If she did what they had agreed, it would be her last disk of pills for a good, long while. She thought for a minute about keeping them from meeting the conditions by dipping into her savings to buy a new, costly wardrobe. The account was in her name, after all; she needn't consult Ted. Really, though, she could delay the pregnancy more sensibly than that. She could tell him that she wanted to wait longer before they had a baby.

Then, though, she would have to tell him why. Even if she trashed her savings account, he would ask why. She did not want to answer. You could tell a guy you didn't love him anymore; you couldn't tell him that you still loved him -- but you loved him less. You certainly couldn't tell him that you were afraid to have a baby with him because you were afraid that you'd love him even less in five or ten years.

And she did want babies. She had been an only child of a single mother, and she wanted four. Ted, who had been the third of four, had warned her that she was romanticizing the experience. "Sure, I want kids. We'll have one, and we can decide about the next after we have some experience with that one."

That sure didn't leave her much wiggle room now. She wanted kids; she wanted Ted's kids. They might inherit his brains, and he would be a patient father. She wanted his kids, and she wanted to raise them with him. She just wasn't sure she wanted to be with him for another eighteen years to do the job.

But, if not Ted, who? She still loved Ted. Thinking that she might someday love him so little that she might want to leave him was no reason to leave him now.

Of course, single women had children every day. So leaving Ted wasn't deciding not to ever have kids. That was stupid, though. She was afraid of having a baby now because she was afraid of raising it as a single mother. She certainly didn't want to leave Ted -- merely feared that she would want to sometime in the future.

By the time that Ted got home, she was eager to see him, so eager that she was already in a sexy nightie.

"Have dinner?" she asked.

"Yeah. I brought you some left-overs if you want them for lunch tomorrow." She carried lunch; his cafeteria was so heavily subsidized that buying lunch at work was cheaper for him than brown-bagging it. Dinner after seven was free. Nothing was too good for programmers who stayed late. "Is it too late?" For sex, he meant.

"I adore Theodore." And, really, she still did. She hadn't used that silly couplet for a while, but it still applied.

"Well, I adore Jessica, too. Give me a few minutes, and I'll prove it." While he was in the bathroom, she took off the nightie. Then she got into bed and pulled the sheet up to her neck.

Ted got into bed without baring an inch of her. Then he leaned over and kissed her before resting on one elbow and slowly drawing the sheet off her.

"It must be Christmas. Santa brought me what I've always wanted." He kissed her again. Then his mouth trailed down to her right breast. His chin scratched, but the scratches were exciting. When his tongue and lips on her nipple had aroused her, she spread her legs. He stroked her cleft until she tensed.

"Ted."

"Yes." He moved over her and between her knees, which she raised. Then he opened her, filled her. "Jess." His chest hair tickled her nipples as he moved above her and inside her. She licked salt from where his neck joined his shoulder. Her arousal gyred upward with each of his strokes. The tension broke, and she thrust herself at him and around him.

"Jess," he said as she clutched around him. "Sssi," as he drove her into the mattress. "Cah!" as he throbbed within her contractions. He collapsed on her, and they gasped into each other's ears.

Somewhat later, he pulled himself off and lay on his side inches away. When she backed into him, he wrapped himself around her.

"You are," he whispered, "the sexiest woman in the whole world." They fell asleep in the spoon, although they woke on their own sides these days. She put the nightgown on and covered it with a bathrobe before cooking breakfast. They kissed lightly before going out the door on their separate ways to their separate work.

It wasn't that Ted ignored her satisfaction, she mused on the commute. He took care to bring her to climax every time. It was just that he brought her to climax in almost the same way almost every time. Ted was a considerate lover -- just as he was considerate about doing his share of the housework and letting her choose her share of their TV shows and her share of their entertainment and socializing. Ted was nice. Was nice enough?

If you enjoyed this sample then look for **Less Than Yesterday**.

MICHAEL FIORI

Step Lovers

Taboo Erotic Romance

"Kids, we are out the door in five -- get a move on!"

The Alberts were hours away from their long-awaited and much needed vacation, and Mrs. Albert was getting nervous that she couldn't hear the rolling of her son or daughter's suitcases on the floor upstairs yet. 'It's probably Hannah making sure she has every one of her fifteen thousand bathing suits,' thought Mrs. Albert as she checked her watch and went through her carry-on in the kitchen.

A moment or two later and she could hear at least one of her children making its way down the stairs. It was Mark by the sound of it -- at around 6'2" and 200 lbs., the solid young man's steps were unmistakable. He didn't need to pack nearly as much, just a bathing suit and some warm weather clothes.

"Rio De Janeiro, here we come!" Mark exclaimed as he rounded the corner to join his mother in the kitchen. His mother thought to herself, what a handsome boy he had become, and he looked it in his sweater and jeans, though he'd obviously need to change into something warmer when they arrived.

Mark's aunt had been suckered into one of those time-share sales pitches and ended up with a few weeks in a beautiful Rio beachfront home that they couldn't make time to use. So when they offered a week to Mark's family, the four had quickly agreed to take the vacation together. Rio de Janeiro was supposed to be beautiful in February, as opposed to the cold winter winds of the Midwest.

When Mark's dad joined his wife and son in the kitchen, it was time to yell at Hannah once again, who replied:

"I'M COMING!" from Hannah upstairs, in an annoyed tone.

Hannah stopped briefly and grabbed the sexy pair of black laced panties she thought she might get to show to one of the vacationing boys she hoped to find there. Her brother would inevitably be staying out late banging some dim-witted college girls as she knew he's used to doing; why couldn't she have a little fun?

High school boys could be so frustrating. Hannah had a few times thought about giving her cherry to a boy she'd really liked, but they'd all disappointed her somehow. Whether it was bragging to their friends, or treating her badly to look cool... every one of them just wasn't worth it. But it was no wonder that they kept pursuing her -- Hannah is a stunner. She had deep green eyes with large black limbal rings around them, which looked almost animalistic when she was scolding her brother. Hannah's thick brown hair looked good straightened, as she usually wore it; or tossed up in a ponytail as it was when she headed downstairs. Her family finally saw her rounding the corner to the kitchen, wearing tight black yoga pants and an equally tight Yankees T-shirt over her 32C breasts.

"You don't even like the Yankees!" exclaimed Mark as his sister came into view. His eyes widened when he saw how little her outfit left to the imagination.

"Oh, shut up, Mark!" She got so frustrated with him sometimes. He was always picking on her, and though she sometimes liked it (it was like flirting practice for boys at school) he often got on her nerves, like now.

Mark couldn't help himself most times, she is an easy target. Plus, it helped him to distance himself in his relationship with his sister. He often felt bad how turned on he got when Hannah's friends came to visit or sleep over. As a senior in college, he wasn't supposed to find their teen bodies and their scantily clad nighttime appearances so arousing. They were his sister's age, and she was a battle herself.

Every so often, Mark thought maybe he could excuse his interest in her, hiding it behind the fact that they weren't 'technically' related. Their parents had married when both he and Hannah were very young, making them step-siblings. But they'd still grown up together, fought and played together, gone to school together... No, for all intents and purposes, Hannah was as much his sister as any of the annoying princesses, aka sisters, his buddies complained to him about. Only most of them didn't have to put up with one like his.

If you enjoyed this sample then look for **Step Lovers**.

WANT FREE COPIES OF MY BOOKS?

Just visit my blog and download free copies of my books:

awesomeauthors.org/justplainbob